Design   David West   Children's Book Design
Editor   Margaret Fagan
Research   Julia Slater
The author, Mandy Wharton Ph.D.,
has taught in secondary
schools and researched into
women's and girls' education.

Designed and produced by
Aladdin Books Ltd
70 Old Compton Street
London W1

© Aladdin Books Ltd 1989

First published in the
United States in 1989 by
Gloucester Press
387 Park Avenue South
New York, NY 10016

All rights reserved

Printed in Belgium

The publishers would like to acknowledge that the photographs
reproduced within this book have been posed by models and have all
been obtained from photographic agencies

Library of Congress Cataloging-in-Publication Data

Wharton, Mandy.
     Abortion / by Mandy Wharton.
       p. cn. -- (Understanding Social Issues)
     Includes Index.
     Summary: Explores various issues of abortion, including the
question of restricting it by time limit, who uses it and why, and
what alternatives exist.
     ISBN 0-531-17189-2
     1. Abortion--Juvenile literature. [1. Abortion.] I. Title.
II. Series.
HQ767.W47 1989
363.4'6--dc20   89-31782
                                           CIP
                                           AC

Contents

Introduction   5
The last resort   7
Case study   17
Abortion in the past   19
Legal abortion today   27
Making the decision   35
Case study   45
The abortion debate   47
Alternatives to abortion 55
Sources of help   60
What the words mean   61
Index   62

ABORTION

Mandy Wharton

Every month many women realize they are pregnant and would rather not be. What are the choices facing them? They could go through with the pregnancy and keep the baby, have the baby and arrange for it to be adopted, or have an abortion (terminate the pregnancy). Many people believe that women should have the possibility of choosing an abortion in certain circumstances but women's access to abortion varies enormously. In some countries all abortion is illegal, in others legal abortion is available up to different stages of the pregnancy. However, it is a "fact of life" that abortions occur, and have always occurred, in every society, whether legally or not.

Modern contraception and safe abortion have been a tremendous liberation for women. Today, in many countries, women have the means to control their fertility and they have the right to decide when to have children. But what rights do they have if their contraception fails, do they have the right to an abortion, should there be an upper time limit on abortions to protect the growing fetus or should abortion be on demand? Abortion is a serious moral issue; some people regard it as always wrong, most think it is justified particularly if it is carried out very early on in a pregnancy. This book looks at the difficult issues of abortion and the debate about its rights and wrongs. It does not aim to give advice about contraception, pregnancy or abortion. If you are worried about contraception or being pregnant you should talk to a counselor, parent or teacher as soon as possible about your worries.

For many people, abortion is an issue of choice so that every child born is a wanted child.

CHAPTER 1

THE LAST RESORT

Many couples share the problem of an unwanted pregnancy. For most abortion is only considered as a last resort when contraception has failed.

Why do women get pregnant in the first place if they do not want a child? Most women do not get pregnant through irresponsibility. Until recently, and it is still the case in the developing world, as well as in most of the Eastern European countries, the main reason why women became pregnant when they didn't want to be was the unavailability of contraception.

Advantages of contraception
Contraception has been a huge liberation for women, allowing them to control their fertility and thereby the pattern of their lives. As women have fought for equality in all spheres of life, they have become unwilling to have their lives directed by their biology. Before contraception was widely available, many women suffered ill-health as a result of many pregnancies and their children's welfare also suffered. But contraception is still not available to many millions of women throughout the world. In some countries women are forbidden by their husbands to use contraception. In many developing countries contraceptives simply are not available due to a general lack of medical facilities.

Using contraception
Even where contraception is readily available, it is not always used. Although the Pill is an excellent method of contraception for many women, it can have side effects. The risk of these side effects compared to the Pill's benefits needs to be weighed and discussed by each individual woman and her doctor. Side effects may be partly why in the United States, only 16 percent of women of

childbearing age are on the Pill. Other methods of birth control also have drawbacks: there is a certain prejudice against contraceptives that interfere with the spontaneity of lovemaking, like the diaphragm or condoms. It seems that many men are reluctant to use condoms. However, this attitude is changing with the spread of AIDS and people are realizing how important it is to protect themselves not only from an unwanted pregnancy but also from the HIV virus which causes AIDS.

Failed contraception
Sometimes contraceptives are not used correctly, or other factors make them ineffective, for example, a severe stomach upset can mean that the Pill's chemicals are not absorbed properly. But generally the Pill's failure rate is only one percent. Occasionally a condom can break. Research shows that if a condom is used correctly and consistently, two women out of every hundred couples using condoms will become pregnant each year. This statistic is also true of the diaphragm contraceptive method. However, with less careful and routine use the failure rate for these two methods of contraception rises to 15 women out of every hundred couples.

> **"I was married with two very young daughters when I got pregnant because of a broken sheath. My husband was livid and told me to get rid of it or he would divorce me and not pay maintenance for the child."** **British woman, 1970**

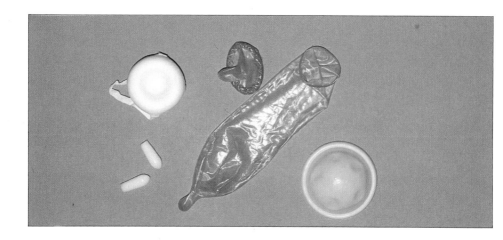

There are many different types of contraception available, and it is very important to seek advice, find one that suits you and learn how to use it effectively. The photograph shows condoms and the cap – the two most effective "barrier" methods of contraception – together with a vaginal sponge and pessaries.

Pressures to have sex

The availability of reliable contraception coincided with a change in people's attitude to sex. The sexual revolution of the 1960s may have been liberating in some senses, but it put pressure on young people to have sex which they were not necessarily ready for.

> **"I went into a drugstore to buy a packet of condoms, but I was too embarrassed to bring them to the counter. Eventually, I asked my brother to get them for me."**
> **Peter, age 17**

In some areas sex education and advice about contraception is inadequate and teenagers do not have the facts about contraception and do not understand the menstrual cycle. On average, girls start their periods around age 12 whereas 100 years ago it was age 16. This means that sexually active and uninformed teenagers are much more likely to get pregnant today than ever before.

"I didn't think you could get pregnant by just having sex once."
Teenager, 1989

Teenage girls who do become pregnant because they don't know the facts may face particular difficulties letting their family know about the pregnancy. Furthermore, they may be unaware of different choices of action open to them and sources of help.

"I eventually blurted it out to my teacher that I was pregnant. We talked about it for a while, and when she said that I could actually get an abortion and took me along to a counselor, I can't describe the relief I felt."
High school student, age 16

Choosing an abortion

However an unwanted pregnancy might occur, the the very difficult decision to have an abortion is not taken lightly. For many it is the last resort in a desperate situation. But some people argue that ever since abortion laws became more liberal, it is increasingly being chosen too readily. Further, women are not facing up to what they are doing in aborting a fetus, and alternatives are not being adequately explored. To understand why many women choose abortion as a realistic solution to an unplanned pregnancy, abortion has to be seen in the context of women gaining more control over their lives. Many women choose an abortion rather than give up their education, work, or long-term plans. Nevertheless, many women who have unwanted pregnancies do choose not to have an abortion. The important issue is that women should have a choice.

Reasons for an abortion – economic hardship
Poverty is one important reason some women choose abortion, but also people want to keep up their standard of living and children are expensive. In the United States a third of all pregnancies are said to be terminated for financial hardship. About 24 percent of abortions are covered by Medicaid (government funded health care) which usually means the woman is on welfare.

> "With my husband unemployed and three children under five, how can we possibly afford this baby? I won't be able to work, and we're already in debt."
> Pregnant woman, age 30

Social reasons for abortion
Having a child, especially on one's own, is a tremendous responsibility. Some women who become pregnant accidently know they cannot have their baby without it causing severe strain. It may be the case that some young girls who get pregnant recognize that they are not ready to cope with a baby on their own and so choose to end their pregnancy. For many women the timing and number of children they have is vitally important. For example, an older woman with several children for whom another child would be too stressful may choose to abort an unplanned pregnancy.

"I had an unstable relationship with my husband, I couldn't rely on him. My mother who had terminal cancer, was living with me. I couldn't face the trauma and upheaval of another baby."
British woman, 1970

More women now work outside the home (yet are mainly responsible for the home). They want smaller families and they want to choose when to have them.

Single parenthood

It is not easy to be a single mother in our society, especially without the support of the extended family. Some women worry about going through an unplanned pregnancy without adequate help and are daunted by the years of single-parenting ahead. Men are no longer marrying their pregnant girlfriends: in 1970 nearly half the single teenagers who got pregnant married during their pregnancy; in 1980 less than one quarter did. Other women fear losing their partner – it is fairly common for men to abandon their girlfriends if they become pregnant accidently.

Many single women choose to continue a pregnancy. Other women become single parents through divorce or bereavement. Single parenthood is for many a rewarding experience.

"A girl? – no thanks"

The above are all social reasons for having an abortion. Another reason for opting for abortion, which is disturbingly becoming more common in some countries, is because the baby is the "wrong" sex. Prenatal sex detection is said to be widely used in Bombay and other big cities in India and the Far East, with abortions being done if the fetus is found to be a girl. If people want fewer children, they want them to be boys – girls are considered less desirable in many societies because they have less economic value than boys.

Fetal abnormalities

With the sophisticated technology of the developed world, many fetal handicaps can be detected. For example, a test called an amniocentesis can detect chromosome disorders, the most common being Down's syndrome. It can also determine the sex of the child. This is important information in the case of diseases that only affect one sex such as muscular dystrophy. An ultrasound scan can detect spina bifida. These tests are done around 18 weeks gestation (18 weeks of pregnancy), and with a positive result a woman may choose not to continue the pregnancy. This will result in a late abortion. Overall, many people argue that a woman has the right to say how much pain and suffering (her own or a child's) she can endure or witness for a lifetime. However, many women continue with their pregnancy accepting the fact that their child will be handicapped. In such circumstances, it is important that the decision is the woman's own.

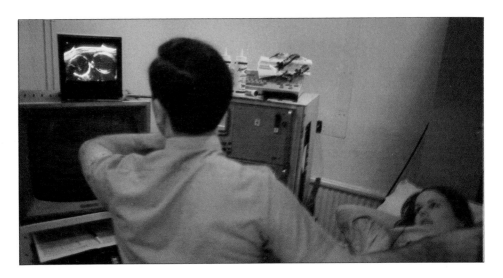

An ultrasound scan done at 18 weeks can detect abnormalities of the fetus' head and spine. It can also be an exciting way for a woman to "see" her baby.

Medical reasons

Many abortions are carried out solely for medical reasons and, for some people, these are less controversial and more acceptable than abortions carried out for social or economic reasons. Medical reasons for an abortion include where the pregnancy threatens the woman's life or where the woman may need treatment for an illness, such as cancer, that will damage the fetus. In these cases the choice can be between saving the mother and saving the child.

"When I was told after the routine scan that my baby had spina bifida, I was shattered. The decision to have an abortion was agonizing, but both my partner and I knew we would not be able to cope with a handicapped child. I felt guilty because I am against abortion, but I had to do it."
Jean, age 25, 1988

CASE STUDY

Shirley and Martin met during their first year in college. Both of them were training to be teachers. They had had other boyfriends or girlfriends before but they hoped their new relationship would last. They often talked about their long-term plans. They felt nothing could shake their feelings for one another.

Shirley and her boyfriend had talked quite a lot about contraception and had been to a family planning clinic for advice. They decided to use condoms as the method of contraception best suited to them. They both thought that they would like children in the future but wanted to find out more about their relationship first.

So when Shirley missed her period and then had a pregnancy test, she was dismayed to discover she was pregnant. How could she continue college with a baby? She just knew that it would be a disaster. Emotionally she was not ready to become a mother and the thought of threatening her career as a teacher was terrifying. Martin tried to persuade her to live with him and have the baby. She was tempted, but asked him if he would provide the time at home which she could not as a trainee teacher. That, of course, was a different matter.

Shirley had an abortion, and felt sad about it but relieved that an unwanted pregnancy would not change her entire life. She resolved to be much more careful about contraception in the future.

Martin was very supportive of Shirley whilst they were deciding what to do. He was very upset though by the abortion – he was quite sure he wanted the baby and felt powerless when Shirley made up her mind about having an abortion. He was fed up by his friends' reactions too when they just assumed he would think of Shirley's pregnancy as an inconvenience. Martin felt there was a lot of pressure on him not to mind about the abortion.

CHAPTER 2

ABORTION IN THE PAST

The photograph shows a British demonstration. Until 1967 access to legal abortion was very restricted in Britain. These demonstrators are concerned that proposed changes to the law will force women to seek illegal abortions to end an unwanted pregnancy.

Women have always made decisions about their pregnancies. It has not been easy for women to prevent or to terminate unwanted pregnancies, but methods have always been available although most of these were extremely brutal.

Traditional methods for abortion
Traditional methods for aborting a fetus have not changed much over time. Formulas for abortion in Ancient Chinese medical books date back nearly 5,000 years, and Ancient Roman medical books 2,000 years old gave advice about how to induce abortion. These ancient methods are still in use in many countries where legal and safe abortions are difficult to obtain, and usually involve substances that are drunk or instruments to scrape out the woman's womb. In China, for example, women drank quicksilver or swallowed live tadpoles three days after a missed period; in India and Africa herbs, sharp roots and massage were used; in 19th and 20th century Britain gin and hot baths, chemicals and poisons, knitting needles and coathangers were used by backstreet abortionists who knew nothing about hygiene. It is difficult to know the success rate of these methods, or the proportion of women who died from infection due to dirty instruments or poison, but we do now know that it is extremely difficult to dislodge a healthy fetus in these ways without doing serious damage to the mother.

Desperate acts
Whether women choose to have an abortion or not, they may be driven to desperate solutions.

The Ancient Greeks and Romans practised infanticide (killing a newborn) by leaving the baby out in the open to die of exposure, and in Ancient China babies were drowned, especially girls who were considered a burden on the family. In Britain thousands of newborn babies were abandoned, for example, in the year 1775 a foundling hospital admitted 10,272 abandoned babies, only 45 of whom survived. Today in Latin America and Africa babies are abandoned on a large scale and many do not survive.

Changing attitudes toward abortion
Although the methods of abortion may not have changed much, society's attitudes toward it certainly have. The Romans believed that the fetus was part of the woman's body and that she could try to remove it if she wanted.

Generally, attitudes toward and laws about abortion have always been influenced by religious beliefs and the official churches. For hundreds of years the Roman Catholic church tolerated abortion before "quickening." This is the time that the mother begins to feel the baby move, and was thought to be when the soul entered the baby. Interestingly, the church taught that for the male fetus this happened at 40 days and for the female at 80 days. The Roman Catholic church changed its teaching on abortion around the early 19th century, and is now extremely restrictive. Many of the Protestant churches have been more tolerant than the Catholic church on abortion. Islam teaches that the soul enters the fetus around 120 days after conception and that after that abortion is murder.

Therefore Islam is tolerant of abortions before this time, and actually states that there must be an abortion at any time if the mother's life is in danger. Buddhism contains no idea of the human soul, but is against killing any form of life. Therefore Buddhists believe that the seriousness of aborting the fetus increases as it grows. The

Attitudes toward abortion have always been influenced by the church. The Roman Catholic church is strongly against abortion. But how many women are involved in its decisions about doctrine? Would the churches' law be different if women did make decisions?

woman's life always comes first. Orthodox Jews believe abortion is immoral. However in a recent survey in the United States 98 percent of Reform Jews said that abortion should be a private decision between a woman and her doctor.

The end of tolerance

Thus although abortion was not approved of and was sometimes punished, it was usually tolerated. This changed at the beginning of the 19th century. Until then, all countries under British law, of which there were many, tolerated abortion at least until quickening. The laws were tightened up and late abortions became punishable by death. The changes occurred for a number of reasons, partly because of changes in Catholic teaching and, partly due to the growth of the Puritan movement. In the United States it was also outlawed because of the high proportion of people dying in the hospital after surgery. Abortion was made illegal because it was not essential surgery. Furthermore, by the middle of the century the medical profession, which was struggling for status and control over medical practice, tried to criminalize abortion as a means of driving midwives out of business.

The earliest law about abortion in the United States was made in New York in 1829. This only allowed abortion if there was a threat to the mother's life. Most European and developing countries followed the lead of the United States in tightening their laws. Legal abortions became difficult to procure and illegal abortions more common. Furthermore, restricted access to abortion was coupled with a restriction on birth control and women often took desperate measures to control their fertility. There are many horror stories about women trying to make themselves abort, or paying illegal "backstreet" abortionists.

"I went to the hospital to terminate my pregnancy, but they said "No." I begged them, as this is my tenth child. If I had $26 I could've got it done by a woman, but who would have that amount of money with all my children?"
Letter received by abortion reform group, ALRA, 1950s

Liberalizing the laws

At the beginning of this century, women began campaigning for the right to control their fertility, and the first family planning clinic in Britain was opened by Marie Stopes in 1921. The first country to legalize abortion in modern times was the Soviet Union in 1920, where the new socialist government saw it as a woman's right. Scandinavia liberalized its laws in the 1930s. Other countries, for example Yugoslavia and France, made abortion legal in cases of rape, fetal handicap and threat to the mother's health. In the United States women's groups set up the National Association for Reform of Abortion Laws (NARAL) in 1932, and the Abortion Law Reform Association (ALRA) was set up in 1936 in Britain.

The two world wars had the effect of liberalizing attitudes further. Once the appalling effects of the Hiroshima atomic bomb on fetuses became known, abortion was seen by many as a humane choice. Governments were under pressure to make abortion more available. A similar pressure came when the effects of the Thalidomide drug, given routinely to pregnant women from 1957, became obvious in 1962. Even with the likelihood of having a severely handicapped baby, women who had been on the drug were refused abortions.

"I was offered Thalidomide when I was carrying my third son. Sometimes I was tempted to take it but never did. But when I thought about what could have happened, I joined ALRA."
Woman speaking in 1963

Another important development that helped change attitudes was a medical breakthrough in the 1950s, when two Chinese doctors developed the vacuum aspiration method of abortion. In this method the contents of the womb can be carefully sucked out and only minimal use of instruments is required. This, and advances in the earlier detection of pregnancy, made abortion safer and easier.

In the 1960s attitudes toward sex and contraception became more liberal. The Abortion Act passed in Britain in 1967, was a watershed which influenced the law in many other countries. Under this law a woman has the right to an abortion if two doctors agree that either her own, or her family's, physical or mental health would suffer by going ahead with the pregnancy.

Most children born while their mothers took Thalidomide are now grown up and lead full lives. Will our attitude to handicapped people be even more stereotyped if all abnormal fetuses are aborted?

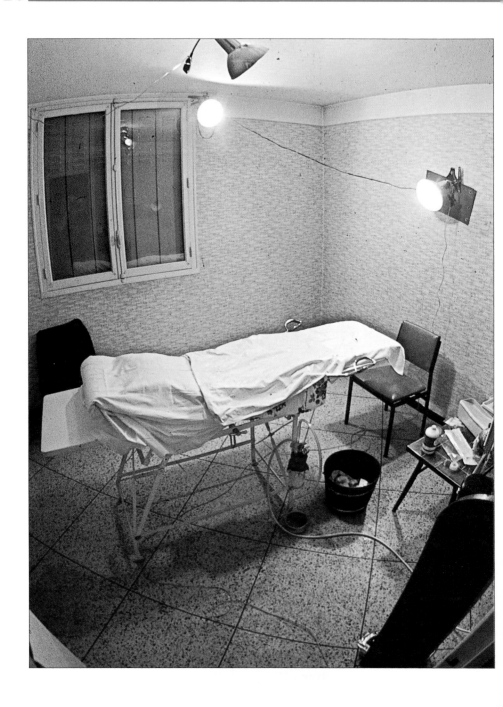

CHAPTER 3

LEGAL ABORTION TODAY

Many women in the world now have access to safe, legal abortion in a hospital or clinic. Yet, the World Health Organization estimates that 200,000 women die each year from illegal abortions.

Laws relating to abortion are dependent on many things as we have seen. In Ireland (Eire), for example, abortion counseling as well as abortion is illegal because of the influence of the Catholic church. In China there are very liberal laws because of the tremendous problem of overpopulation: on the other hand Romania has very strict laws because the government is worried about underpopulation. Other socialist countries tend to have liberal laws as they uphold the right of women to control their fertility. But in every country there may be conflicting forces and hence much debate; for example in socialist Nicaragua the Roman Catholic church has a strong influence and abortion is illegal.

Liberal laws
In those countries with a more liberal law, the state acknowledges that women do have a right to make a decision about abortion.

"I have always agreed with the anti-abortionists that life begins at conception, that doing an abortion is not the same as removing an appendix. I wouldn't like to live in a society where people saw abortion as like having a cup of tea. Women find it an agonizing decision, but they have the right to make it."
Wendy Savage, obstetrician, 1988

In 1973 Denmark became the first country in Western Europe to allow abortion on request in the first three months of pregnancy. France, Italy,

Holland and Sweden also now have abortion on request in the early weeks, although the time limit varies from country to country. These liberal laws result in very few late abortions and much less trauma for the woman. The socialist countries of Eastern Europe also have liberal laws, except for Romania where the pressure on women to have children is great. It has been reported that in Romania those with less than four children have to have examinations every month to check that they have not had an (illegal) abortion.

The United States laws vary from state to state, but in 1973 a Supreme Court ruling gave women the right to terminate a pregnancy, in consultation with a doctor. However, although abortion is easily obtainable, no federal money is allowed to be spent on abortions or on abortion counseling. Until recently, most states provided money for poor women, but there was a backlash against abortion and now 40 states will not provide cash help. In Britain, the 1967 Abortion Act made abortion legal up to viability, that is when the fetus is able to live outside the womb, on several medical and social grounds. In 1929 viability was determined to be 28 weeks. The Act does not apply to Northern Ireland, where an abortion is more difficult to get. At the present time Singapore has the most liberal law in the world, as a woman can have an abortion on request up to 24 weeks gestation.

How many illegal abortions?
It is estimated that there are 40-60 million abortions in the world each year, about half of which

are done illegally. It is obviously very difficult to be accurate about the number of illegal abortions, but estimates can be based on the numbers of women admitted to hospital because of complications due to illegally induced abortions. The World Health Organisation (WHO) estimates that 200,000 women die each year after illegal abortions. Questionnaires can also help us know the extent of illegal abortions, although women do not always admit to having had one.

> **"On the first day of the month my high school is empty. All the girls are at home waiting for their welfare checks. There are 13 and 14-year-olds walking around the corridors pregnant."**
> **New York high school student, 1975**

How many legal abortions?
It is easier to keep track of the number of legal abortions. The abortion rate, that is the number of abortions per thousand women of childbearing age, varies from country to country. Some extremes are the Soviet Union, where it is estimated that on average a woman will have 6-10 abortions in her life, to the Netherlands where the rate is relatively low: abortions are easily available in both countries but contraception is virtually unobtainable in the Soviet Union. Twelve percent of American women, and less than three percent of British women have more than one abortion.

It is interesting to look at some of the statistics for England, Wales, and the United States. There are about 1.5 million abortions a year in the United

States and about 170,000 in England and Wales (about 14 percent of these are done on women from other countries, especially Ireland and Spain.) The rate in the United States is more than double that in England and Wales, and many more abortions are carried out on teenagers. This is due to the lack of contraceptive use rather than any difference in sexual activity. It is estimated that 27 percent of American women of childbearing age do not use contraception: 7.4 percent of these said they were sexually active – 9.25 percent were under 24.

Talking to her partner or friends is important when a woman is making up her mind what to do if she is pregnant. Talking to a doctor or clinic is also helpful as they can advise about a legal abortion or support her to continue with the pregnancy.

"I have one kid here in the clinic, 17, who's just had her third abortion. It's a desperate situation. Is it right to solve her problems with yet another abortion?"
U.S. counselor, 1980s

Who has legal abortions and when?

About 81 percent of abortions in the United States and 50 percent in England and Wales are done on unmarried women. Ninety-one percent of abortions in the United States and 84 per cent in England and Wales are done before 12 weeks gestation (approximately 12 weeks after conception). In Sweden, where early abortions are easy to get, 96 percent are done during this period. These statistics are important because they show that in countries that allow women access to abortion, it is carried out long before the fetus becomes formed enough to survive outside the mother's womb.

The placards say: "Babies should not be forced to have babies" and "Children deserve more than to be punishment for sex." The protesters are expressing their worry that new restrictions on legal abortion in the United States would mean an increase in the number of babies born to teenage mothers.

Many of the most distressing and passionate arguments about women's rights to abortion occur when late abortion is being considered. In England and Wales, nearly 3,000 abortions a year are done over 20 weeks gestation. But of those abortions carried out between 17 to 19 weeks, 30 percent of the women had been referred before the twelfth week. Also in England and Wales, about two percent of abortions are done because of fetal abnormality or risk to the mother's life, this rises to about 20 percent of abortions over 20 weeks.

Liberal abortion laws and access to contraception tend to be asssociated with developed countries where women expect to be able to control their fertility and have gained a good measure of equality. In these countries, the infant and maternal mortality rates are low. If an abortion is carried out in the early weeks of pregnancy, then there is little health risk to the woman. However, the health risk does increase as the pregnancy continues. There is no doubt that access to safe and legal abortion has contributed to women's improved position in society.

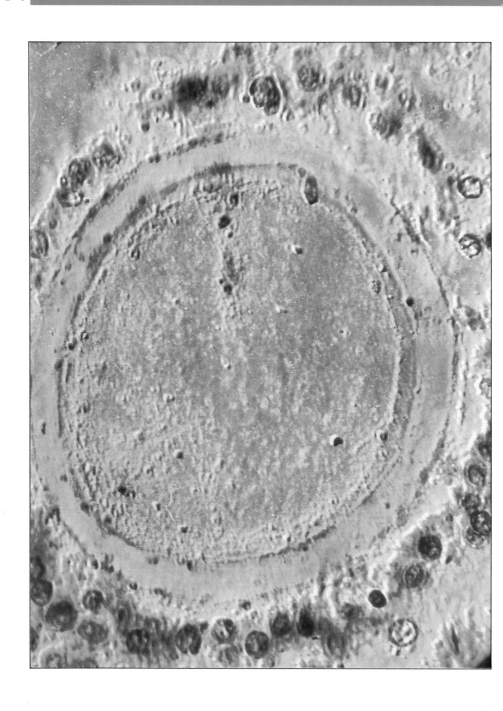

CHAPTER 4

MAKING THE DECISION

The photograph shows an electron microscope picture of a human sperm attached to a human egg. Most people believe life begins here – at conception. Have women the right to make the decision to stop the pregnancy; and and if so until what stage?

What happens to a woman when she discovers she is pregnant and doesn't want to be? Some women go straight to their doctor, others to a referral service which specializes in giving advice about contraception and abortion. Many women seek counseling before making up their minds whether or not to have an abortion or to go through with the pregnancy. Jane became pregnant when she was 17 and did not want to go to the family doctor. She couldn't tell her parents, and felt very alone. Her boyfriend was very supportive and wanted to marry her. But Jane did not want to get married. She decided to go to a referral agency.

Sharing the problems of an unwanted pregnancy is important – whatever the individual woman may choose to do. For some women a telephone call to a referral service is the first step to making the decision about whether to have the child or an abortion.

"The female counselor was great, not judgemental, she was just anxious to make sure that I wasn't being pressured one way or another by other people."
Jane, age 17, 1985

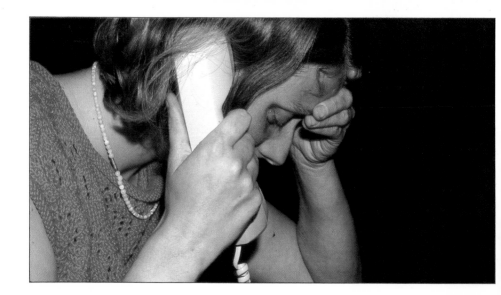

Once a woman has missed a period, she may suspect she is pregnant. Standard pregnancy tests cannot be done for a further two weeks, by which time she may be six weeks pregnant. Home pregnancy tests, provided they are used carefully, can give an earlier – but less accurate – result.

Clinics and family doctors also offer confidential pregnancy testing and can offer support if the woman is anxious about the result. In the United States an abortion can be arranged in an outpatient clinic or doctor's office. The cost is usually $200-$250. Women with health problems or those having later abortions are often referred to hospitals.

> **"When I found out I was pregnant I was determined not to lose a grip on things. I decided to have an abortion and went to a clinic right away. Afterwards I felt sad, but I mainly felt enormous relief that I could get an early abortion. The feeling that the decision was right has stayed with me all these years."**
> **Helen, age 35**

Development of the fetus

In order to understand more about abortion techniques and the moral issues surrounding abortion, it is important to know about how a baby develops in the womb. The age or gestation of the fetus is measured from the date of the woman's last period. An egg is usually released about two weeks after this, that is, in the middle of the menstrual cycle. The normal gestation period for a full-term baby is 40 weeks. If an egg is fertilized, (the point of conception) it takes about a week to travel to and become implanted in the womb, or uterus. Many fertilized eggs fail to do this, and are washed out with the next period.

At four weeks gestation, the various organs and limbs begin to appear and grow and we now talk of an embryo. At about eight weeks gestation the embryo begins to take on a distinctly human form and we refer to it from now on as a fetus. Twelve weeks is considered to be a landmark because at this time the fetus grows very rapidly. It is also considered the earliest moment in the development of the brain where conscious sensation becomes possible. However, it is thought that the fetus is not able to "feel" anything like pain until around 18-20 weeks.

The diagram shows the female reproductive organs. An egg leaves the ovary (2) and travels down the fallopian tube (3) to the uterus (1). Sperm from a man's penis enters the uterus via the vagina (4). The uterus lies behind the bladder.

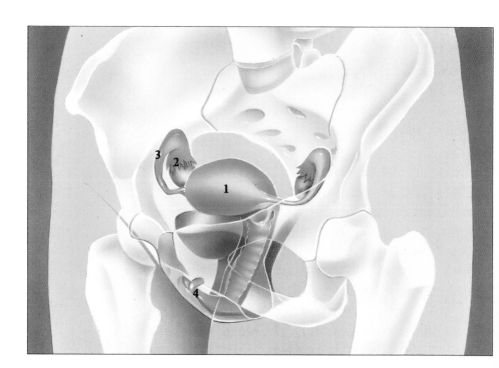

> "I believe the choice should be left to the individual woman… but I also think a woman must be made fully aware that what is at stake is not a clump of inert cells, but the beginning of human life."
> Male doctor

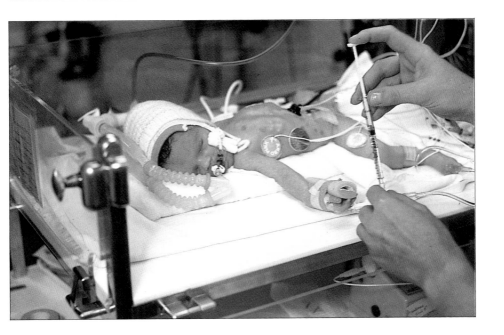

Twenty-four weeks is considered the point of viability, that is, when most fetuses can live outside the womb. Yet few doctors will carry out abortions after 20 weeks. Babies born before 28 weeks that survive are often handicapped, sometimes severely. The likelihood of handicap, however, decreases as time goes on, every day being crucial. It is important to remember these points when considering the moral arguments presented in Chapter 5.

At present, about half the babies born prematurely at 25 weeks can be saved and about one in five born at 24 weeks. There seems to be no prospect in the near future of keeping a fetus of less than 22 weeks alive.

Abortion methods

The methods used for medical abortions vary according to the age of the embryo or fetus, between doctors, and from country to country.

It can be argued that the IUD (intrauterine device) is a method of very early abortion, although it is classified as a contraceptive device. It works by preventing an egg from implanting in the womb. A woman will never know if the egg was fertilized or not when she has her period. Another method classified as contraception is the "morning after" pill, which can be taken up to three days after unprotected intercourse. This series of pills is a high concentration of hormones that brings on a period, flushing out any fertilized egg. These are relatively uncontroversial methods as there is no certainty that there is a fertilized egg, let alone a viable pregnancy. The French have just developed an abortion pill that can be used up to eight weeks after conception. Called RU486, it usually brings on an abortion. However, it does not always work and will affect a surviving fetus, so surgical methods may be needed as well.

Early abortion

There are two methods of very early abortion available to women who know they are pregnant. One is called endometrial aspiration and can be used up to seven weeks gestation. No drugs or anesthetics are needed – the contents of the womb are just syringed out. Another method is the use of prostaglandin pessaries which bring on a "late period." Both these methods require that pregnancy is detected in its earliest stages.

The most common method of abortion, used up to around 13 weeks, is the vacuum aspiration method performed under local or general anesthetic, where the contents of the uterus are sucked out. Afterwards, the uterus is lightly cleaned out with a curette.

Second trimester abortions

In the United States, second trimester abortions are also performed using the vacuum aspiration method. Yet, at this stage, however, instruments are used to help break up the fetus to draw it out. Then the uterus is cleaned with a curette. Many hospitals use this method up to 19 weeks.

In Britain the procedure differs. The woman's cervix is dilated, the fetus is removed with forceps, and a D & C is given. This method can only be used up to 17 weeks, however, because of possible danger to the cervix.

A fetus during the third month of development. The photograph shows how the umbilical cord connects the fetus to the woman's placenta. In the third month facial features start to develop as do fingers and toes.

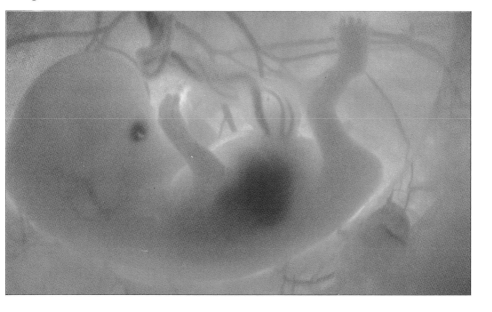

A late abortion is normally done through labor induced by prostaglandin. Labor can take anything up to 36 hours and is like a normal labor – but the baby is stillborn. A D&C is sometimes given afterwards.

There are advantages and disadvantages of a prostaglandin abortion. It is much less damaging to the cervix which expands slowly, and no anesthetic is necessary. On the other hand, such an experience can be extremely painful and very distressing.

More unusual methods
There are other methods of abortion which are extremely rare. A hysterotomy is like having a caesarian section, and a hysterectomy removes the whole womb, usually when there is cancer.

> **"Yes, right up to the abortion I felt it was wrong – both morally wrong and against my body's wishes. But the circumstances were all wrong."**
> **Single young woman, 1984**

Reactions to abortion
Women's responses to having an abortion are very varied, and cannot always be predicted. Women who have had little support can easily become depressed. Some therapists would say that depression comes from not acknowledging and mourning their aborted babies. For some women, it is very difficult to admit to having had an abortion, partly because of the fear of moral disapproval, but also because it is a subject that causes embarrassment,

like miscarriage or death. In Japan, a high-rate abortion society, couples place small dolls at a Buddhist shrine as a memorial, and this helps the grieving process.

Women's most common reaction to abortion, however, is one of tremendous relief that they are no longer pregnant.

> **"It wasn't traumatic, it was just a relief. I've had no regrets, no depression – I've hardly thought about it since."**
> **Woman, age 24**

The implications of being pregnant when not wanting to be and giving birth to an unwanted child are often so awful that for many women the realization that she does not have to bring the pregnancy to term can produce tremendous relief. Most women need no post abortion counseling and pick up their lives happily and go on to have children later when they are in a stable relationship and can plan for a child.

What about the feelings of others involved in an abortion? Abortion can contribute to the breakdown of a shaky marriage or relationship but it should be remembered that having children, especially unplanned ones, can also put tremendous strain on a relationship. Parents of young girls often feel failures and blame themselves if their daughters accidently become pregnant. They either feel guilty that they did not talk to their children about sex and contraception or feel that they have somehow "gone wrong" in bringing up their children.

"When my father found out I was pregnant he threw me out of the house. It took my mother two weeks to persuade him to let me come back. I had an abortion, and no one has ever mentioned it since – that was very hard."
Hazel, age 17, 1989

In general, doctors agree with liberal abortion laws, but not with abortion on demand. They want to be involved in the decision.

Nurses are in closer contact than doctors with women having late prostaglandin abortions and they are required to give lots of support. Staff in abortion clinics can suffer emotional burnout. In general hospitals nurses do not have to work on abortion wards.

On the other hand, medical staff working with abortion patients often find it deeply rewarding. They are seeing people in trouble get a second chance to put their lives back together.

Father's rights

At present in most countries the father of the child has no rights over the decision to have an abortion, although he may influence it. Some attempts have been made in the United States and in Britain to change this, so far unsuccessfully. Many men do not want their wives or girlfriends to have an abortion. They can feel a deep sense of loss after the abortion yet still believe that a woman has the right to choose.

CASE STUDY

Patricia is 20 years old. She worked hard throughout school and had always looked forward to having a career. When she started nursing school she felt a great sense of achievement. Her studies were almost finished when she discovered she was pregnant...

It was rather embarassing when, as a single student nurse working in a hospital, I discovered I was pregnant. It was my final year, and although nobody actually talked about it much, there was the general feeling that I would be getting an abortion. That's what I felt too, after all, I wasn't in a steady relationship and wanted to concentrate on my nursing career.

I think working with patients made me think much more deeply about it. I had seen a lot of distressed women, not just those having abortions, but also the ones losing their wanted babies through miscarriages. Anyway, I decided to go through with the pregnancy. Everyone obviously thought I was crazy, except one nurse who told me that she had been adopted. Perhaps she imagined that her mother chose not to have an abortion and was thankful. Managing a career and being a single-mom is difficult. But I've been extremely fortunate. My mom and dad, although they were horrified at first, have helped a lot and so have many of my friends. When Kate was born and I realized the amount of work involved in looking after a new baby, my spirits slumped. Gradually, things eased up and I was able to arrange shared child-care with a friend of mine who lives nearby.

Perhaps the hardest part of being a single parent is being so poor. Without some help from my parents I think the situation would have been really grim. I didn't expect finding boyfriends would be easy either, but a couple of years ago I met Adrian who has made a great effort to accept Kate. I've never regretted my decision to say "no" to an abortion. When I look at my daughter I'm so glad I stuck out for what I think is right.

CHAPTER 5

THE ABORTION DEBATE

The banner reads "protect unborn children" and these women are protesting against the current abortion laws. They believe that life begins at conception and that abortion is the murder of an unborn child.

There is a whole spectrum of opinion about whether or not, and for what reasons, women should be allowed abortions, until what fetal age, and whether women have the right to choose to end a pregnancy without medical permission. This chapter will consider the debate mainly as it is in the United States and Britain. Hopefully, the historical and statistical information in the earlier chapters will help you to make up your own mind about this controversial issue.

Opinions on abortion

Most people accept abortion in certain situations. In the United States, for example, only about 10 percent of adults feel that abortion should never be permitted, while 25 percent feel it should never be forbidden. Less than half approve of abortions for social reasons only.

> **"There should be real medical reasons. Contraception is readily available. Adults should take some responsibility for their actions."**
> **Woman doctor**

The majority are overwhelmingly in favor of aborting a defective fetus – there is much support for infanticide of the newborn severely handicapped as well. During the latest attempt to change the Abortion Act in Britain, a survey showed that although most people believed women should have access to abortion, there was a narrow majority in favor of a time limit well below 28 weeks.

These are the opinions of the general population, but many individuals have much more extreme views and campaign vigorously for them. The debate has become polarized, with extreme positions on both sides blurring the debate in the middle. This means that it can be difficult for the majority of people to clarify their views.

The popular view

The most commonly held position is a "gradualist" one, whereby the rights of the fetus increase as it grows until they equal those of the mother. Therefore counselors should help the woman in making her decision either to carry through the pregnancy or arrange to have an early abortion. From the gradualist standpoint, once the fetus becomes viable, it should not be aborted.

The placard says "Our bodies, our lives, our right to decide." Each attempt to make access to abortion more difficult has been met with demonstrations from people who believe in a woman's right to choose abortion.

The extreme anti-abortion argument

The most extreme anti-abortion argument comes from the Roman Catholic church. They are against abortion for any reason and are also opposed to the IUD. Others hold this extreme position without being Catholics, and many Catholics hold more liberal views despite the teaching of their church. In the United States, the National Right to Life Committee, the leading anti-abortion group, was founded in 1970 and today it has over a million members. Sixty-seven percent of the membership is female.

> **"Every fetus has a right to life. We cannot take that right away."**
> **Clare, single parent**

In the United States there are various anti-abortion groups: the well-known National Right to Life Committee and the more extreme Operation Rescue. These groups argue that life begins at conception. Usually they describe the fetus as "the unborn baby" regardless of the stage of its development. Anything that threatens that life, be it the IUD, the "morning after" pill, or abortion, is murder.

A woman's right to choose

> **"A woman should be able to demand an abortion whenever she wants it, without having to plead or apologize or justify herself to doctors."** **Julie, 1986**

On the other side of the debate in the United States is the National Abortion Rights Action League (NARAL) whose aim is to protect the woman's right to safe, legal abortion. Many religious groups support NARAL, such as Catholics for a Free Choice. In Britain the feminist National Abortion Campaign (NAC) was formed in 1975. They felt that a woman has the right to choose an abortion with no time limit; that women should have access to abortion on demand. Extreme feminists argue that as a fetus is part of the woman's body, she has the right to decide what to do with it. This position led some women to leave NAC because they held a more gradualist position.

Feelings about abortion run high and many women are willing to risk imprisonment to get their message across. This woman is restrained by the police for trying to stop women going into an abortion clinic.

An upper time limit?

For many people the main issue about abortion is the upper time limit at which it can be carried out. Modern technology has complicated the issue. It would be much easier if we could still believe the old maxim that life begins at quickening but we now understand much more about fetal development. A fetus born at 25 weeks or more has an improved chance of surviving unhandicapped – should the mother be the only one to decide about her baby's life at this stage? If a potentially viable fetus is aborted after 23 weeks, is that any different from infanticide? There is some sympathy for allowing severely disabled fetuses to be aborted this late, but what of those few late abortions which are carried out for social reasons? Should we be allowed to kill our newborn babies if they are not convenient for some reason, or is there a difference between late abortion and infanticide?

The needs of society

In some areas of the world, like China, the need of society to control its population influences the country's attitude to abortion. Indeed, infanticide was quite common until recently. On the other hand in Latin America, thousands of babies are abandoned because of poverty and abortion being illegal due to the influence of the church on the state. It seems too that if the state does interfere with a woman's choice about whether or not she can have an abortion, the consequences of this refusal are lasting. Studies in Czechoslovakia and Sweden have shown that the children of women who were refused an abortion tend to perform less well at school and to be in trouble as teenagers, when compared to children from wanted pregnancies.

Weighing the rights

Who is to determine the rights of all those concerned in each individual case? How do we decide when, if ever, the "rights" of the fetus are greater than those of the mother? What of the father, or the doctors involved – what are their rights? To what extent should the overall needs of society dictate the options available to an individual woman? These questions all need to be asked. They are not easily answered, but the debaters should consider all the issues before adjusting the scales of the availability of abortion.

Advanced technology means many fetal abnormalities can be detected and the mother offered an abortion. But do we want to create a perfect "super race"? What are the "rights" of the handicapped fetus? This Downs Syndrome child obviously enjoys life and brings joy to her mother.

CHAPTER 6

ALTERNATIVES TO ABORTION

Both men and
women need
to take
responsibility for
contraception.
Using
contraceptives
carefully is the
best alternative
to abortion.

No society likes abortion, and the main task is to enable women to avoid becoming pregnant when they feel it is wrong for them to have a child. Contraception, education, and an enhancement of women's self esteem and status in society are the keys to women being able to make free choices about planned parenthood. If we are worried that the availablilty of abortion makes it an "easy option" which will make our society less caring and less moral, we must consider the difficult situations many women find themselves in and change those.

After all, single mothers are the largest group of people living below the poverty line, and there is still a social stigma against them. People caring for the handicapped do not get the financial help or emotional support they need and this adds to the particularly difficult decision to continue the pregnancy of a handicapped fetus.

Adoption
One alternative to abortion is adoption. Before the 19th century adoption and fostering was practiced on a casual basis throughout Europe. In some societies, for example in the Caribbean, formal adoption was never necessary because the family accepted all children. During the 19th century in the developed world, there was increasing prejudice against children born outside marriage and single mothers. As attitudes became more liberal, adoption, this time on a formal basis, became more acceptable. After the Second World War, adoption increased rapidly in Britain and peaked in 1967 with 25,000 adoptions. Since then there has been a

rapid decline, and the demand, especially for newborn babies, enormously exceeds supply; in 1986 there were less than 2,000 babies available for adoption. Meanwhile there are 96,000 older children in care in Britain with very little hope of having any family life. The main reason for this decline in the number of newborns for adoption is the liberal abortion law.

"The baby was kept in the hospital overnight and then we all met in the office and I was able to meet the baby's new parents. They were lovely people."
Single mother, 1970s

Adoption can lead to deep and fulfilling relationships. Most adopted children are very happy but do feel the need to learn about their natural parents.

A real alternative?

There is a general attitude in society that it is wrong and too traumatic for a woman to go through nine months of pregnancy and birth and then "give away" her baby through adoption. It is certainly the case that there are many tragic stories of the way young women were treated in the 1950s when they were basically forced to give up their babies for adoption. But have we gone to the other extreme – adoption is rarely put forward as a serious alternative when counseling women with unwanted pregnancies. With proper support and counseling, a woman may prefer to go through a pregnancy and give up her child for adoption.

Other alternatives

A more long-term way of reducing abortion figures might be to aim to make the family less isolated again, to try and make the community more responsible for its children so as to take the burden and stigma away from single mothers. The state has a role to play here too, providing adequate childcare facilities so that single mothers can go out to work and not get caught in the poverty trap.

> "I'm glad I went through the pregnancy. Being a single mom isn't too bad, but then I'm lucky I have a great deal of support both from my family and friends."
> Lucy, 1989

Conclusions

If we agree, as most of us do, that abortion should be legally available, and that women have the right to play a large part in the decision making process, then we should also make sure that contraceptive knowledge is improved, and contraceptives are freely available, that it is easy to get an early abortion if that is the decision made, and that a woman has *real* alternatives to abortion. We also have a duty to make the issue one of public debate, and not to leave it to extremist positions. It is a public responsibility to create the conditions in which women will choose courses of action that are seen as the most desirable and responsible.

> "Sometimes I just feel this tremendous relief that I belong to a generation that can control their own fertility safely. It is a great freedom to plan a career and a family and to be able to do it with one's partner." Mary, age 30

At the center of the abortion debate are the rights of the fetus and the mother. At five months a fetus has all the features of a baby, but it cannot yet live outside the womb without intensive medical care. In order to make decisions about abortion, society needs to prepare young people to think about when it is right to have sex and to have children. Everyone needs to know about planned parenthood.

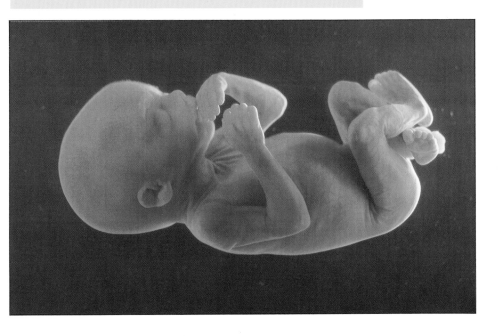

USEFUL ADDRESSES

Clearinghouse on Women's Issues
1819 H Street, N.W.
Washington, D.C. 20006

This is a clearinghouse for information on women's issues.

Planned Parenthood Federation of America
810 Seventh Avenue
New York, N.Y. 10019

They operate 750 centers throughout the country which provide medically supervised family planning services and educational programs.

FOR FURTHER READING

Abortion (Opposing Viewpoints series). Series Editor Bonnie Szumski: Minnesota: Greenhaven Press, 1986.

Abortion: Facing the Issues, by Susan Neiburg Terkel: New York: Franklin Watts, 1988.

Abortion Policy: An Evaluation of the Consequences for Maternal and Infant Health, by John S. Legge, Jr.: Albany: State University of New York, 1985.

From Crime to Choice The Transformation of Abortion in America, by Nanette J. Davis: Connecticut: Greenwood Press, 1985.

Reproductive Rights and Wrongs: The Global Politics of Population Control and Contraceptive Choice by Betsy Hertmann: New York: Harper & Row, 1987.

WHAT THE WORDS MEAN

abortion the explusion of the contents of the womb before the 28th week of pregnancy

AIDS Acquired Immune Deficiency Syndrome. Caused by the HIV virus that can be transmitted through sexual intercourse, AIDS is usually fatal. At present there is no cure

amniocentesis a test done around 16 weeks gestation where some fluid is taken from the womb. Some abnormalities, as well as the sex of the child, can be determined from this fluid

contraception a way of preventing pregnancy

embryo term used for the developing human during the first eight weeks of pregnancy

fetus after eight weeks the embryo is called a fetus

gestation the weeks of pregnancy

infanticide killing a baby, usually before the baby is one year old

menstrual cycle the cycle of producing and releasing an egg.

If the egg is not fertilized by a male sperm, it will be flushed out with the lining of the womb that had prepared itself for a fertilized egg. This shedding of the womb lining is called a period. Women's menstrual cycle is usually 28 days but it can vary enormously

miscarriage, or spontaneous abortion where the contents of the womb are expelled before 28 weeks of pregnancy through natural causes

Pill developed in the 1950s, the contraceptive pill changes the hormone balance in the woman's body and prevents the production of eggs

sterile for a female, unable to become pregnant; for a male, unable to father children (infertile is a more usual term)

trimester three month time span

ultrasound a technique that allows the fetus to be seen on a screen. It does not involve X-rays, which can harm a fetus

INDEX

abortion, illegal 23, 28, 29, 30
abortion, late 32, 42
abortion, laws 21, 23, 24, 25, 28, 29, 44
abortion, methods 40, 41
abortion, traditional 20
abortions, numbers of 30, 31, 32
adoption 56, 57, 58
AIDS 9, 61
amniocentesis 15, 61
anti-abortion 50

cap 9, 10
condoms 9, 10
contraception 5, 8, 9, 10, 30, 36, 40, 56, 61
councelling 36, 43, 58

D&C 41
diaphragm 9
disability 52

embryo 38, 61

family planning clinic 24
father 44, 53
fetal development 52
fetus 5, 11, 15, 16, 20, 21, 32, 37, 38, 48, 49, 50, 56, 61

gestation 32, 37, 38, 61

handicap 15, 24, 39, 56

illegal abortion 23, 28, 29, 30
infanticide 21, 48, 52, 61
IUD 40, 50

menstrual cycle 37, 61
miscarriage 38, 41, 43, 61

periods 10, 37, 40
Pill 8, 9, 61
poverty 12, 56, 58
pregnancy 5, 12, 14, 15, 16, 33, 36, 40,

48, 56, 58
pregnancy testing 37
prostaglandin 40, 42, 43

religious attitudes 21-22, 51
rights 5, 53

sex 25
sex detection 15
sexual revolution 10
sterile 61

trimester 41, 61

ultrasound 61
uterus 38

vacuum aspiration 25, 41
viability 39, 52

womb 20, 25, 38, 40, 41
women's rights 5, 15, 32, 48, 50

Photographic credits:
All the photographs are taken with models and obtained from the following agencies:
Cover: Associated Press (both); pages 1, 5, 7, 8, 9, 10, 11, 16, 17, 18, 19 and 21: Rex Features; pages 2, 12, 13 and 20: Science Photo Library; page 3: Network; pages 4 and 6: Vanessa Bailey; page 14: Sieveking/Network; page 15: Abrahams/Network; page 22: Popperfoto.

PRINTED IN BELGIUM BY

proost

INTERNATIONAL BOOK PRODUCTION